The Christmas Proof

Tenesha L. Curtis

Astanna

This is a work of fiction. Names, characters, organizations, places, events, and incidents are either products of the author's imagination or are used fictitiously.

THE CHRISTMAS PROOF
Copyright © 2024 by Tenesha L. Curtis

Published by Astanna, an imprint of Writerwerx University.

Astanna.com

Paperback ISBN: 978-1-961891-02-9

eBook ISBN: 978-1-961891-01-2

Cover and book design by Tenesha L. Curtis (TeneshaLCurtis.com).

Editing services provided by
Kimberly Hunt of RevisionDivision.com
and
Michele Kessel of MicheleKessel.com.

Paperback version printed in the United States of America.

The Christmas Proof

Tenesha L. Curtis

Table of Contents

1

The massive construction worker walking through the automatic doors doesn't seem to hear or feel the sickening crunch under his Red Wings.

"Dammit," I whisper, waiting until he gets a few feet ahead of me to bend and pick up the sad pile of white wooden letters that used to be my name badge. I try to shrug off my irritation. No sense getting worked up about it.

"What happened?" Tory's voice sounds through my earbuds. I hear my best friend clicking her mouse rapidly, so I sense she is checking emails from her boss even though it's ten minutes until six on a Friday night.

"I dropped my name badge, and it fell under this guy's boot. I'll have to ask Vanny for another one." I put the shattered K-A-S-A pieces in my jacket pocket and continue into the store. The badge-destroying man heads left toward the frozen foods. I turn right toward the customer service desk.

Pinpoints of golden light pull my gaze toward the ceiling. Drone lightning bugs about twice the size of their organic counterparts are the latest addition to our inventory in time for Christmas. Since I'm always on dayshift, I don't get to see the iridescent-winged bots in their full glory. They are now executing their pre-programmed flight patterns near the entrance in plain, tantalizing sight of wide-eyed children and curious adults waiting in line at the check lanes. Vanny's idea. And the shrinking pyramid of drone boxes near the floral department proves it is a genius one.

The Foothills IGA is an excellent example of a small-town grocery store. We have a lot to offer—from eggs to phone chargers to tampons to roses—and it's all snuggled up into a shop less than the size of some gas stations. Big Canoe is a North Georgia mountain community at the tail end of the Appalachians. I grew up here surrounded by beautiful views and tourists rotating throughout the year for business retreats, class reunions, romantic getaways, and family vacations. Though there are smaller retailers like convenience stores and dollar stores sprinkled around Big Canoe, IGA is the only convenient "real" grocery store. The next nearest is a shopping area with a Kroger and a Walmart more than ten miles away. We get a lot of "quick run to grab" traffic.

As it is on the first day of every month, the store is bustling. It's busier now because it's the first of December. People are here for their normal groceries using their monthly benefits deposits or to stock up for the month so they don't have to come back down the mountain for a few weeks. But there are also people getting money orders for cash gifts, buying turkeys and hams to prepare for Christmas dinners, and applying for our new IGA Visa cards to bulk up their budget so they can shop for more (or better) presents for their loved ones.

"I've told Vanny before that she makes those letters too thin. They're cute, don't get me wrong, but not durable. She slices the wood until it's like paper." I can hear Tory typing now. If she starts another project for the law firm she works at, she'll be hanging up soon, which is fine since I'm about to clock in.

"No, it's fine. It's my fault. The pin's been wonky for a couple of weeks. It must have been loose and slipped off my vest." I should have told Vanny the first time it started acting crazy, but I thought I was leaving the store soon. Why did I need a new name badge for a place to which I wasn't coming back?

To the left of the world's shortest customer service counter is a tight hallway with a time clock. I put my index finger on the clock, and the surface flashes green as it records my start time as 5:52 p.m. I turn around to wait for Vanny to finish cashing a customer's check so I can ask her for a replacement badge. The ends of her jet-black hair curl slightly at the top of her shoulders, and her smile is warm and genuine as she counts hundreds into the elderly woman's hand. Vanny likes to make all our name badges, painting them herself. No plastic or instant label makers for her team. It's adorable, but cumbersome and time-consuming. This makes me feel more guilty for not fixing the pin earlier. Worse, because I shouldn't work here anymore.

"I just clocked in," I tell Tory, hearing her typing growing faster by the second.

"And I just got another assignment, House. So I need to go, too."

I laugh. I'm sure she's thrilled to have the firm trust her so much. She doesn't need to go—she's *dying* to go.

"Okay. I'll talk to you later."

"Sure thing. Have fun!"

She disconnects the call. I put my earbuds in their case and slide the container into my vest pocket. A few seconds later, I get the habitual text warning me to stay away from Dillin. I roll my eyes and smile, typing a quick Yes, ma'am and wishing more than anything I was in Atlanta with her.

"Evenin', Kasa!"

"Hey, Kasa!"

"Kasa, sweetie, you're still here!"

I wave and nod at the greetings from my doctor, the girl who works in floral, and a popular real estate agent who lives nearby. It's still wild to think that a couple of weeks ago, the IGA staff had a "City Slicker" going-away party for me on my "last" day. It was complete with a cake shaped like downtown Atlanta's Bank of America Building. I'd been so excited and so proud to be getting away from the slow-paced, tranquil mountain life in Big Canoe.

Like Tory, I would live in a big, exciting city and make a new life for myself at the ripe old age of twenty-three. Everyone else who moved away did so in their middle or late teens. Tory held out until we were twenty; I was her only reason to stay. She had saved up the money for the move by working at the IGA deli. She had researched work opportunities in law. She had compared housing rentals until she established her career enough to afford something more substantial.

Seeing her do this while I stagnated, I had no choice but to push her toward her destiny. The last thing I wanted was her resentment or thoughts that I'd held her back from something. After all, we are only an hour's drive apart. I convinced Tory to go by framing her departure as a way to settle tand do some experiential recon. That way, she could help me plan my relocation to Atlanta. A good, true friend who loves me will do as I ask, right?

As Vanny hands the customer a receipt, she turns to me and I show her the shattered letters cradled in my hands. "I'm so sorry."

"Just dump it," Vanny says, twisting her thin, tan lips in annoyance and rolling her brown eyes. "I'll make you another one tonight." She turns to another customer approaching the counter, waving a dismissive hand at my quick, "Thank you."

I drop the pieces in the trash below the time clock and start down the hallway to the breakroom so I can put my keys and wallet in my locker. As I walk, I take an adoring look at the beautiful man on my phone's lock screen: smoldering amber eyes, sepia skin, onyx locs framing his angular face. Is it possible to fall in love with someone you've never been in the same room with? If so, I've done it. Hard.

Reave Alami has been my favorite author since I stumbled upon his debut epic fantasy, *The Time Drinker*, in middle school while we were on a class trip to the Pickens County Library. I've always loved dark blue and his novel was a beautiful midnight color with a metallic sheen to it. My thirteen-year-old brain had to have it, mesmerized by the way it seemed to pulse in the light as I walked past. When I was satisfied that the cover didn't reveal anything scary—I never could handle horror well—I flipped it over and saw his author's headshot. It was teen-hormone-fueled-attraction at first sight. Marginally more fascinating to me than his face was his being seventeen years old according to the bio under his picture. I was so impressed that I started to get it into my head that *I* could be a young author. After all, he was only four years older than me. And I liked reading books, so why couldn't I write them?

As never before, I started putting a real effort into the creative writing assignments that were part of my English classes. Where I had previously begged to do verbal stories instead of written ones, I shocked my teachers by submitting written fiction without argument. But I noticed that when it came to the creative side of things, I didn't have the best mind for storytelling. I'd get a few exciting pages out and then lose interest in writing the story, having to slog through to the end of something only a few thousand words long. I wanted it done for me so I could read it. No way could I write an entire novel. Who had time for all that world-building and character-development business? And then there was *re*-writing on top of that? No thanks.

But the attempt gave me more respect for what he was able to do with a laptop and twenty-six letters at his disposal. Without putting a finger on me, this man moved me—to tears, to anger, to lust. To dream. His main characters were almost always female, and they had a subtle, self-assured badassery about them. They'd do everything to prevent a fight, but once the enemy crossed that line, the heroines would subdue the enemy without breaking a sweat. They wouldn't initiate an encounter with a love interest, but if they got a hint of desire, they dove into sophisticated seduction that would turn hard-to-get into begging-for-more.

So of course, I had to start a fan club for him of which I'm still president. Reave Needers now has over 10,000 registered members. That's more than 10,000 people who are as fascinated by Reave as I am. Finding a favorite author is a great thing, but being part of a community of other people who love him almost as much as I do is heavenly. The only thing that would be better is meeting him, face-to-face, in the flesh. But I'd probably run and hide if that ever happened, as I get uncomfortable in most social situations.

Sometimes I feel like those main characters in the early portions of his books. I've never quite gotten to the "badass" part of my life—leaving the nest, making my way in the world, coming into my own. But Reave pushes me to never forget that I'm headed there. To stay the course. If I ever get to meet him, I have to try to pretend I know how to speak and thank him for keeping me focused and inspired.

Day to day, I don't live my life like his heroines do. But leaving Big Canoe will be the start of who I'll be in the future. Kasa+. The kind of woman Reave writes about in his books. Someone brave and bold who takes the world by the throat and submits it to her will. Someone who lives life based on her desires and not what other people want from her. There's even a chance I could find someone like Reave to be my partner in that kind of life. I'd feel like a billionaire if I could find romance with somebody half as amazing as Reave.

And who knows? Maybe I will. One day.

"Hey there, Fingers," a familiar, pre-pubescent-sounding voice comes from ahead of me, dragging me from my hopeful thoughts of Reave and the future. I look up to find Dillin, one of our baggers, approaching me with a face pocked with pimples and a smile dying for a set of braces. Not much has changed with him in the past six years since we left high school. He's still a bagger at the IGA. He still hasn't gone to college. He still hasn't moved away. We have a lot in common and that is both sad and comfortable. And comfort is trouble. Exactly the kind of "settling" I don't want. I have to get out of here. I have to do more. *Be* more. Soon.

"Hey, Dillin," I mumble, nodding to him and trying to slide past him into the break room.

"Hold on there, now," he says, holding a palm right in front of one of my breasts, daring me to move into his touch. I stand still, looking at a swirl of blonde hair hanging above one of his eyebrows.

"Everything okay?" I ask.

"Yeah, yeah," he says, lowering his hands to my waist, baby blue eyes mischievous. I stiffen. We are not ten feet away from Vanny. Her suspicion of what we sometimes do on her property is different from her seeing us touching like this with customers in view. "I was wondering if you could help me with something in the back. It'll be really fast, I swear."

He leans close as if he's going to kiss me, chapped pink lips curved up and parted, and I can smell whatever he ate. Something spicy and dripping with dumpster juice.

"Yeah. Sure," I say and follow him to the back of the store, fiddling with the keys in my pocket and taking another longing look at my phone. What I wouldn't give to have Reave be the one taking me to the stock room. The thought makes my head spin with all the delightfully naughty things I hear from Tory's sexual adventures, read about in

Reave's books, and see on Pornhub.

A notification momentarily blocks my view of Reave's eyes. It's another message from Scammereave. This guy messages me a few times each month through the Reave Needers website. For years he's claimed he's the real Reave, expecting me to fall for it. I read his messages because of how oddly positive they are. This one says Fantastic job with the text-based Q&A with the AJC. You made me sound like a master of the craft. It made me blush. Keep up the awesome work. I appreciate you. And as always, a custom winking emoji made to look like Reave's face.

As I finish reading it, I realize I'm blushing now. I wish this guy were the real deal. What would it be like to have a private place to chat with Reave one-on-one? Would the real Reave be this kind and flattering all the time? Surely he would. And I wouldn't mind that flattery bleeding over into the bedroom where so many of my fantasies about Reave have taken place. With Reave, I would be adventurous. Assertive. And I believed that he would let me be. I'd try anything and everything until I found out what I liked the best. Though, I have a short list of things I want to start with.

Just not with Dillin.

For him, sex is all about *him* getting off. If I were to derive any pleasure from it, that would be purely coincidental. Only once in six years has he tried eating me out. I was pleasantly surprised that he asked. Then insanely disappointed with his "effort." It was like he was filing taxes or washing dishes. He wasn't excited about pleasing me; he was fulfilling some kind of obligation or repaying a debt. He stuck to slow, random licks in odd spots with little force, as if he wanted to be as far away from me as possible, yet still have me magically orgasm. He sighed six times before I told him he didn't have to keep trying. I don't think he could have looked more relieved if I told him a jury had acquitted him of a triple homicide.

With a shrug and a "We tried, right?" he sprinted back to his living room to play video games while I got dressed in his bedroom and left shortly after that.

I look up in time to catch the stock room door swinging outward after Dillin walks past it and off into a corner out of sight. He waits for me to catch up, unbuttoning his pants. Blow jobs were his favorite, but after a co-worker nearly caught us, he decided hand jobs were easier to hide and abandon if someone walked in on us.

Tory has been telling me since we were in high school that I need to get away from Dillin. Part of me knows I should. The other part has trouble letting go of what's familiar. Whatever his motives might be, he's consistently interested in me beyond friendship. And again, there's comfort in that, regardless of how he acts or what he looks like. And what he asks of me isn't exactly draining. A few hand jobs in the back of the store every month. Who cares? Ringing up groceries takes up more energy than two or three minutes of jerking him off.

It is nice to feel wanted, even by him. I have a loving set of parents, and Tory's been my right hand since elementary school. So it's not like I don't get any connection or closeness with people. But when it comes to sexy stuff and guys, the ones I want don't seem to know I exist. And the ones who want me, the Dillins of the world, are tolerable but don't take my breath away. Not like the couples

Reave writes about.

Tory found real love with her fiancée, Allana. A notorious nap addict, Tory didn't sleep for two days straight after their first conversation. She knew then that she needed to do whatever she could to convince Allana—who had sworn off all romance after a gruesome divorce from her high school sweetheart—to take a chance on love for Tory's sake. Tory had to have her.

No one "has to have" me. They'd take me if it suited them at the time. They'd tolerate me if they had to. But the ability to fathom life without me? No. No one but my parents and Tory. Even though we aren't a romantic couple, Dillin would at least notice if I wasn't around and maybe miss me as a sex partner.

He takes ninety seconds this time. What else is there for me to do but count? No one up front would have time to notice we were gone. Dillin's fingers are under my shirt, pinching my nipples like he's going to tear them off my body. I try to disguise my pained face as a smile. I keep my fingers seated at the base of his dick, letting his cum spurt onto the floor between his sneakers so I'll have less to wash off myself.

"Good job, Fingers," he pants, patting me on the shoulder after releasing my breasts. All I can muster is an "Okay" as I scurry away, putting my bra back in place and heading to the employee restroom to wash my hands. I know Tory would be disgusted and confused to know what I'd done (again), but I feel an unsettled relief. I'm glad it's over and appreciate him asking me. Is that pathetic? Maybe. But what else is there? Barely 3,000 people live in Big Canoe. There are over 6 million in Atlanta Metro. I'll have a much better chance of finding my version of Allana there. Maybe even the fantasy version of Reave that lives in my head. This thought makes me genuinely grin as I tear a paper towel from the roll to dry my hands before heading back to the break room as I'd intended before starting my shift. Once I leave Big Canoe, I'll be able to become someone new and sophisticated like Tory with her paralegal job, her long hours, and her wrist-straining engagement ring.

"All yours," the cashier I'm relieving says as I wait for her to log out and take her cash drawer with her. I insert the drawer

Vanny handed me, put my phone on top of the till next to the monitor (allowing me to discreetly read any texts from Tory or Reave Needers notifications), and start ringing up a man impatiently waiting for the end of our changing of the guard. I step into the fray for the next few hours. One thing I can say about cashiering is it keeps my hands busy and allows my brain to wander. Not that I wouldn't rather be busy with one of Reave's novels, a hot mug of tea, and a thick blanket. But, as far as working goes, I could do a lot worse.

The amount of robotic lightning bugs I'm ringing up pushes my mind toward the engagement rituals of the Kortanians from Reave's latest book, *The Flavor of Magic*. He based the ritual on the idea that illuminating the entrance of a lover's abode shows you are offering yourself up to be the one to light your way home. The characters in the book use everything from glass bowls filled with creatures reminiscent of angler fish to huge dung fires enclosed in towers of mud. That handmade or manually-gathered brightness is a powerful, bold show of devotion for that race of humans.

"You're still here," Nurse Donova's voice drips with frustration as she steps up to the register with a cart filled nearly to the brim, pulling me out of autopilot. She tied her thinning, ivory hair in a ponytail, the end of which licks her brown, leathery ear every time she turns her head. At almost six feet tall, she is still an imposing figure as she nears seventy. I haven't seen her since the going-away party when she dropped off a keychain with an enamel book ornament for the keys to my first place in Atlanta. "I figured you would've hired a professional house sitter—like I *told* Himari, mind you—and shuffled on down to join Tory by now." She narrows her emerald eyes at me before I turn my focus down to her order, needing to look away from that stern, Cherokee face.

"No, ma'am. I'm waiting until my parents get back from Europe." Eggs, ham, key in the code for bananas.

She pauses with a can of beets in her hand, and I look up to see her give me her patented "don't be an idiot" look before continuing to pull items out of her shopping cart.

"Kasa, you're an adult now. I

understand that. But you've given enough. You stayed here through your mother's diagnosis, the treatments, *and* her recovery. You should have been gone what? Five years ago? You gave that up for her, and that's what any good daughter would do. But now it's *your* turn."

I nod as I scan a bottle of grape juice and a can of pears.

She sighs.

"Himari told me she gave you plenty of money for your move after your Uncle Yuto died and left her all that cash. So you have the financial resources to go, don't you?" She nods to the man who steps in line behind her, and he waves back.

"Yes, ma'am," I mutter, wrapping two Christmas-themed mugs in paper bags before sliding them down the lane toward Dillin.

I don't want to talk about this. Or rather, I don't want to hear her lecture me about this. But asking her to stop feels disrespectful to her as someone older than I am, my former school nurse, and a customer that I'm currently serving. But she was never the type to ask if someone wanted to discuss something. If she wants to bring it up, that's exactly what she will do—even if we are alone in the store. That would be torture. But her saying all this in earshot of other customers and fellow employees is excruciating. She's right. I am an adult, and she has no right to talk to me this way.

"Your Uncle Yuto being racist toward your parents is plenty of reason to take every cent he left, *that son of a bitch*," she hisses, hefting two jugs of whole milk onto the belt, her anger giving plenty of power to her thin, buckskin-clad arms.

I know that. I thought *haafu* was some weird Japanese nickname my uncle had given me for the first few years of my life. When I told kids at school about the nickname, word got back to my parents. Mom had to explain that it meant "half"—more accurately, "half-breed"—and that he was using it as a slur for my Mexican-Japanese heritage, not a nickname. That was the first time I'd ever felt rejected and insulted in my life. Unfortunately, it wouldn't be the last.

"So you deserve to take the bastard's money and go hog wild! Move to Atlanta. Buy a library full of books. Hell, buy your own bookstore. Isn't that right?"

I nod again, and Dillin chimes in with a too-loud "Damn straight!" This earns him a poke in the ribs and a glare from Vanny as she walks by on her way back up to the customer service desk. My heart feels like it shakes my whole body with each resonant beat. Anger heats my insides, but I try to keep my face neutral. I'm certain her ability to sense what she used to call "sass" hasn't dulled over the years, so I try to avoid appearing as if I have profanity on my mind.

A third customer joins the line. Either those gallons of milk are colder than I realized, or my palms are slick with my sweat. Texas toast, inhale, garlic aioli, exhale, key in the code for red seedless grapes, don't cuss out Nurse Donova.

My phone lights up and vibrates against my till as a Reave Needers notification comes through. Her eyes move to it for a second before she puts her last item on the belt and pushes her cart down to Dillin's waiting hands.

"See! You're still managing the fan club for that famous author. Get an office space in Atlanta, and run it like a real business. Make a name for yourself doing something you love to do."

She pinches the bridge of her broad nose and shakes her head before digging her wallet out of her purse as I tell her the total. Now Nurse Donova is chastising me. I've irritated her, but it's not like any of this is her business. I know she's concerned, but did she have to say all that out loud right now? None of it's a secret, but it's not something I'd talk about with Dillin or with customers around, even if there are two others in line right now.

When I offer her her change and receipt, she takes them but wraps her umber fingers around my wrist.

"I love you, Kasa, but *please leave*. See what else is out there. I've seen what happens to kids like you when they stay here too long," her derisive side-eye in Dillin's direction is quick as lightning, "and I don't want that for you. Himari and Rio don't want that for you either, though they're too timid to say. That's where you get it from, I guess. If you go and hate it for some reason, then you can always come back. But *go* first."

She releases me with a sad smile, thanks Dillin cooly, and pushes her full cart out of the store. I start to calm down as I begin checking out the next customer.

When Mom told me about what Uncle Yuto had left us and handed me a check to cover all the help I had provided with her medical bills while she was in and out of the hospital, there was part of me that wanted to rip it up. A very small, very stupid part, but it was there. The more rational end of my brain knew better. Tory had been able to leave Big Canoe in a reasonable amount of time because she worked and saved for it. We both knew that we would need money for a deposit on a place to stay, that we'd need to be able to get utilities turned on in our names, and that we might not be able to get steady work for a while, so having some financial padding of at least a few months' rent was essential.

On every trip I've taken to Atlanta, seeing the sheer size of the homeless population has made me terrified of running out of money. I know I can always come back home, or even ask my parents for more, but the thought of failure is still awful. Seeing that Tory made it the past few years is soothing, but only slightly. With Uncle Yuto's money erasing the fact that I had used all the funds I earned to help my parents stay afloat, moving to Atlanta was as accessible as if I had saved every cent I'd earned since high school. But I didn't see any reason to not add more insulation between me and living on the street—okay, maybe asking for some cash from Mom and Dad—once I moved. I figure if I'm going to be here another month anyway, why not take an easy job and stack even more money on top of what I already have? I forgot about the part where Big Canoe residents know my business and some aren't afraid to share their opinions on it. But at least I won't be staying for long.

My parents will be back on the first of the year. I'm leaving the next day. For real this time.

I check my phone—a different, randomly selected photo of Reave's handsomeness displays there now—to see we have twenty minutes left until closing, along with another message from Scammereave with only a heart emoji. He's never sent something like that before. It's pleasant but startling. Following my usual protocol, I don't respond.

There are one or two people still looking around the store, but I take my chance to grab my favorite holiday treat: Santa Cheese. I need something delicious to give me a little dopamine spike after work. Santa Cheese comes in a glass sphere. The two halves unscrew after you remove the slender, golden label that seals the seam. The label displays the brand name in a crimson, Vivaldi script (yes, I looked it up). Uber Christmas-y. The cheese inside mixes several of my favorites. Goat cheese is delicious on its own. But the brand creates confetti of large chunks and small bits of roasted red bell peppers, green onions, smoked paprika, and tarragon. And the bit of granulated garlic and white pepper they season it with kicks the tastiness up another notch. I know for a fact that I can order it on Amazon without it having to be in season. But there's something about buying it from our quaint little IGA and taking it up the mountain on my way home that feels like a mini tradition.

As I walk over to the dairy cooler, I realize that this month will contain the last few times I'll buy Santa Cheese as a resident of Pickens County. This time next year, I'll be living in Brookhaven, Kirkwood, or even Virginia Highlands. I plan on visiting my parents periodically, and likely during the holidays, but I'll be a Fulton or DeKalb County resident then.

I reach for what I see is the last of the Santa Cheese, a lonely little sphere of glass in the corner of the shipping box, but something big, soft, and warm touches my fingers first.

It's a hand in a black leather glove. My eyes move up the lean arm coated in inky wool. Then I see the face from which a rich, all-too-familiar voice emanates while I stare in stunned silence.

"Oh, excuse me, I..." he begins but then stops when he sees my face. His lips remain parted and they are as kissable and luscious as they are in all his pics. Though he's stopped speaking, the bass of his voice is still reverberating through my body, like it does during a podcast interview. I touched the hand of the man who created the worlds and characters that made me who I am today. Well... who I plan to be tomorrow, anyway.

Reave Alami is in *my* IGA and, apparently, he also likes Santa Cheese.

2

I can't feel my heartbeat.

I think I must be actively dying from the shock of what's happening. But I don't miss—as a matter of fact I relish in it—the movement of his eyes from the comfortable shoes I'm wearing for long stints of standing up to the brown, loose curls knotted at the top of my head, and finally back down to my eyes. And his pupils are *massive* in their rings of amber. Reave being attracted to me at all is some kind of fluke. But looking at me like that in IGA casher mode is a full blown miracle.

Finally, I find my voice.

"Sorry, I...you can have it. I'll go get ready to ring you up," I say as I turn on my heel to leave.

"Wait," he says and it comes out breathy like he's as aroused as he looks. Like we've already been in bed together. I stop in my tracks and almost melt when I feel him close the distance between us, hovering over my back. He's a foot taller than me and I feel every inch of the difference. I don't know that I've ever been this close to someone I am so infatuated with. I mean, how can you not fall for someone when you love the creativity that comes out of them? That shows you who they are. Their mind and soul. Their essence.

I try to remain as calm as I can, but the pulsing between my legs and the racing of my heart and the sensation of him so close behind me that I can smell him make that a losing battle. The scent reminds me of moss or dew. Something forest-like that makes me want to take a deep breath of him. He reaches around me and places the Santa Cheese in front of my belly.

"I insist," he says quietly, right next to my ear, which has to be fiery red at this point. "That the most beautiful woman I've ever seen get what she wants."

It's like someone dumped a pot of

scalding water over my head. Is Reave Alami—*THE* Reave Alami—flirting with me? A grocery store cashier?

I deduce that I'm asleep. There's no way this is happening in real life. That's too much coincidence, too much luck, for me to have in a single day. But shouldn't I have woken up by now from seeing him? Would I be able to hear him so clearly and smell him so strongly if this were just a fantasy?

The glare Vanny has directed at me is what certifies for me that this is really happening. She sees me in the dairy section facing the front end, but not actually at my post. Another customer has placed their items on the belt and looks like they're fishing coupons out of their tote bag. Vanny shoots me another wide-eyed, warning look.

Now my hands tremble as I take the sphere, mutter my gratitude, and step away from him to get back to doing my job. It's like leaving a warm fire to go hike in a blizzard. What I wouldn't give to turn back around and climb him like the sexy statue that he is. But Vanny is telling me with her eyes that my job is on the line if I don't pick up the pace. If I wouldn't feel so guilty about it—especially during the holiday rush—I'd quit right now. If I had more courage, I'd ask him to come home with me tonight.

But, unlike Tory, I haven't gone through a series of one-night-stands and half-hearted dating relationships before falling for Reave. I have no practice with flirting. Dillin tells me what he wants and I do it. Beyond Dillin, the closest I'd come to any kind of tryst was ogling attractive strangers jogging past my house during their weekend stays. And I never spoke to them, just watched and daydreamed. I'd been too sacred. Always too afraid. Pining after Reave from afar was much easier than trying to start anything amorous with the few prospects in and around Big Canoe. If anyone had ever asked me to date them, I would have jumped in with both feet. So far, Dillin had been the one and only guy to even come close. And any real romantic relationship between us is nowhere on his radar or mine.

But once I get away from Big Canoe—and my all too knowledgeable community—and start living on my own terms, I'll gain the confidence I need. I'll just walk up to a guy and ask if he wants to fuck just because I want to fuck him. He won't have to approach me, or ask me anything.

But today, I am not that girl. And definitely not when it comes to Reave fucking Alami in the smooth, clean-shaven flesh.

Right now, I'm just going to ring up groceries and try not to vomit.

As I approach the register and mouth an apology to Vanny, who grunts and goes back into the office, I slip the cheese onto the shelf under my till. When I finish ringing the customer up, I wish them a good weekend and turn to find Reave facing me, pulling items out of his hand basket.

"G-good evening. Did you...find everything okay tonight?" I stumble over the spiel I've said at least ten thousand times, but keep my head down, just focusing on pushing the items across the scanner. Half-loaf of wheat bread, cherry jam, almond butter.

"I found everything immaculate," he says, pulling even more blood to my face. "Thanks for asking, Miss..."

I glance up to find him looking at

my chest. A huge turn-on for me. Then I realize he's looking for my name badge.

"Sorry. I'm Kasa. I'd break you. Ah! No! I mean, my badge. I broke my name badge that's why I don't have one right now. Sorry, sorry."

He chuckles and the sound makes me want to dive across the conveyer belt and tear his clothes off. What is *wrong* with me?

"Well, thank you, Kasa."

Reave Alami just said my name. Reave Alami is within arm's reach of me.

Hand quivering, I start bagging up his order and tell him his total. My stomach drops when I see Dillin returning from gathering carts in the parking lot. Before he gets to the register, and while Reave is removing his gloves and concentrating on the card machine, I sneak the Santa Cheese into one of his bags.

This falls far short of the gratitude I wanted to verbalize if I ever met him in person. To tell him how inspirational his work has been for me, what it's meant for me throughout my life when things got hard. The escape it provided that saved me from reality when I needed it the most. But this delicious ball of cheese is all I have to offer right now.

"Evenin' sir," Dillin says as he steps up to the end of my check lane, gathering and aligning the handles of Reave's bags as his receipt jets out of the printer.

"And to you," Reave replies, taking the bags from Dillin and nodding thanks. I turn and grab the receipt, folding it neatly to hand to him. Tory would insist that my number be on the back of it, but it would be too obvious to write it now. Especially with Dillin all of three feet away. He can get jealous pretty quickly if he sees someone talking to me in what he thinks is an overly friendly way, let alone a flirtatious one.

"For the record," Reave says, sliding his long thumb over my palm while I try to remain standing and conscious, "I think you taste great. Oh. I am so very sorry. I meant you *have* great *taste*. Ya know. In cheese." He holds my gaze for an extra second, giving my hand a squeeze that has a ridiculous amount of heat to it for such a small gesture, before pulling the receipt, and his hand, away.

"Watch it, gramps. You can't talk to her like that," Dillin says puffing up his bird chest. I can usually see the signs of his dander getting up, but I was too immersed in Reave to do anything of the sort. Now it's too late. Now Dillin is either going to get his ass kicked and get fired, or at least he'll make Reave think pursuing me is too much trouble with a loose peashooter like Dillin around. He's going to ruin it. This tiny bit of a fantasy that I get to live for a few short minutes.

For the first time since I've known him, I *hate* Dillin.

I feel it surging up through my body. I want to hit him, scream at him, anything to get him to shut up and leave Reave alone. Leave *us* alone. But I'm at work. And no real harm has actually been done. And, realistically, I know that there's no way that a man like Reave would really me. He may be attracted to me, and that might even fuel a bit of kind flirtation, but would he actually have sex with me if given the chance? Absolutely not.

But the face that Reave makes in response to Dillin isn't offended, angry, or even abashed. He looks at Dillin with pity on his face.

"Hmm. Someone's cranky," Reave says and turns back to look at me as he walks past Dillin like he's furniture,

"Mama Kasa, make sure the little one doesn't stay up past his bedtime again. He might have a better attitude in the morning."

And then he winks at me and I'm hovering somewhere between fainting and laughing myself to death at the look frozen on Dillin's face. By the time Dillin works through his shock and takes a step forward, Reave is already through the outer set of automatic doors, waving casually without looking behind him.

"Let's get one thing as clear as your skull," Vanny says, popping up out of nowhere and putting a palm to Dillin's chest as she looks up into his face. "If I ever see or even hear about your disrespecting a customer like that again, you're done. Do we understand each other?"

"But he was—!"

"I," Vanny steps forward and Dillin backs up haphazardly, his spine hitting hard against the end of my check lane, "asked you a 'yes' or 'no' question, Mr. Rankin."

"Yes," Dillin growls and then slides out from between the hard metal and Vanny's angry face to start collecting trash. He grumbles under his breath as he empties the bin under the time clock.

"Are you two official now or something?" she whispers to me, concern on her face. She, too, is not a fan of Dillin's. Like Tory, her heart would probably stop if she thought Dillin and I were a legitimate couple. I'm still reeling, trying to catch my breath.

"No. Uh...he just gets...territorial? Possessive? Possessive sometimes."

"Well, that guy's always been a customer who could've taken me home," she lifts an eyebrow. "Did you get his number? Give him yours?"

"I guess I don't really need to. It was...it was Reave."

Vanny mouths his name, eyebrows nudging together like she's trying to remember where she's heard it before. "Oh! The guy who's fan club you run?"

Her eyes begin to widen, the nature of the situation dawning on her.

"Wait," I say, "You said he's always been a customer?"

"Yeah. You always used to work mornings, but he only comes in here at night. At least once each week. But only in July and December for some reason.

I never asked him." She shrugs. "Just as well. If he's a writer, he'd probably just bore me with book talk." She gives a fake cringe and comes to pat me on the shoulder. "How are you? That must have been huge."

"It is. I still can't believe it happened. And...I swear he was *flirting*. With *me*."

Vanny laughs. "Because men flirting with beautiful women is absolutely outlandish." She gives an exaggerated look of shock before turning serious. "In my experience, if you think he was flirting, he was. And he may be back! So remember not to waste the opportunity next time. Do..." she tosses her hands up and wiggles her fingers "...whatever you kids do nowadays when you want to get in somebody's pants."

It's wild to me how easy everyone makes this seem. Like you can just walk up to someone you've been salivating over for nearly half your life and ask them to have sex. Though Tory would likely tell me that's exactly what she would do in the same situation. Hell, I know for a fact that she has done that on multiple occasions. If I expect to live a life like hers and be comfortable in doing so, why not start now? Vanny's right.

As I hear Dillin scream in frustration as he exits to the rear of the store, I realize that *that's* why I don't jump into things like this. At least not in Big Canoe. There are too many people like Dillin and Nurse Donova around here who have known me for most, if not all, of my life. They've changed my diapers or taught me in school or played spin the bottle with me or given me life advice when I made a mistake. They've watched me grow up. Shifting gears on them— what will probably look like—out of the blue seems unfair somehow. If I'm going to start acting like a different person, I need a new environment to do these new things in. Or at the very least, someone who isn't a lifelong Big Canoe resident to do them with.

And wouldn't Reave be a hell of a practice run for Kasa+?

I try to put my thoughts back on my work like they're supposed to be. Pulling my credit card app up on my phone, I ring up a miscellaneous item, charge the price of Santa Cheese ($10.06 with tax) and pay for it. Then I take the till to the office for Vanny to count. When she comes to help me sweep, mop, restock, and sanitize the front end, I tell her about my gift to Reave and listen patiently to a mini-lecture about shrinkage. Then she praises me for doing something more than just "stalking" the man online.

Dillin does the rest of his work as quickly as possible when he has to do it near us. I'd always heard that the end of the night could be fun and gave the closers a chance to get to know each other better. While Vanny and I seem to be doing that, Dillin just wants to leave as soon as possible. When he finally storms silently out the door, not even waving goodbye to me or Vanny, my stomach drops. I feel guilty. Even though Dillin and I are not a couple, I don't owe Dillin anything, and there was no way I could have predicted or prevented Reave from showing up tonight, I still feel like it's my fault that he's so mad.

Vanny jolts me out of my thoughts by placing something cold against my cheek. I yelp but turn to see that delicious orb of dairy I crave.

"Santa Cheese!" I say, giggling like I'm a teenager again. "I didn't think you'd open another box until tomorrow. Thank you!"

"Thank yourself. It's coming out of your check!" Vanny says, handing me my new name badge as well. She sticks her nose in the air and makes a sweeping motion with her hand toward the door, like a queen dismissing a member of her court. I grin, give her a bear hug, and then move out into the parking lot so she can set the alarm. We say our goodnights in front of the building and each get into our cars.

As soon as I pull my door closed, I text Tory a microscope emoji. That's our code for something major happening that we really need to dig down into. Whenever we're struggling with a tough choice, or something insane happens to create a story so long and / or convoluted that texting won't do it justice, we just send that emoji. The other person then needs to get themselves situated and carve out a decent amount of time to process the event.

By the time I make it up the mountain, it's raining. Luckily, the worst of it doesn't hit until I'm actually in the house.

The home I grew up in has a cozy

feel created by a massive log front and a wrap-around wooden porch that my dad built himself. With three bedrooms and two stories, it's not luxurious, but it's always been plenty of space for us. The front door opens onto a landing where you can leave your shoes and coat, which I do. I slip my feet into the set of thick cabin socks I always leave hanging on the wall. There are two levels to the house and a split stairway right at the front door. On the right are the stairs that descend to the lower level. Down there are two large bedrooms that share a small common area in the middle and a lower-level patio. One is my room. The other is a library and tribute to all things Reave Alami that any stalker would be proud of. I'd always been afraid that I would mess up his books, figurines, or posters while doing things like getting dressed or having a dance party with Tory in my room. So all my Reave paraphernalia was housed in the spare bedroom. To the left, stairs ascend to the public areas of the house and the master bedroom. I go upstairs and pass between the living room and dining area to round the corner into the kitchen.

By the time Tory calls me, I have a mug of lemon-laced hibiscus in one hand and the Reave Needer's app open on my phone in the other. There's another message from the Scammereave, telling me a post I'd scheduled to be published during my shift had made him laugh. I can't help but grin while I read the note and see the trademark wink emoji that looks just like Reave's face that closes the message. I scroll through other messages as I ponder just how psychologically unhealthy it would be to just pretend that the messages from this pseudo-Reave were from the real one. I also consider the idea of telling all the Reave Needers that I spotted the real one today. But I've kept my identity a secret ever since I started the fan club, and I don't know that revealing myself now would have any benefit.

At first, my father made anonymity a stipulation of me creating a fan club for Reave at all. He didn't need some crazy person hunting his daughter down or trying to kidnap her from school. I didn't know who in the world would go through the effort of trying to kidnap me from a school that was essentially on a mountain summit, but I didn't argue the point. Being as shy as I was back then (and am now, for that matter), the idea of doing this with full anonymity wasn't anything I was going to be upset about. So I have an entire online persona across various social media platforms and through the fan club website where I am known as "Katacru." Unless you knew that my full name was Kasa Tanaka Cruz, it'd be hard for you to figure it out from those letters. It looked to most people like some kind of gibberish word I'd made up, so I'd been safe all these years. The fan club's ten-year anniversary is coming up in May. The idea of asking Reave to do something special for this milestone event crosses my mind.

Then I laugh at myself. I failed to even ask the man for his number, but I'm going to ask him to do the fan club a favor?

"Tellmetellmetellme!" Tory says the second I answer the call.

I walk her through everything that happened between this call and our last. I reiterate the fact that in every interview where the subject has come up, Reave stated that he had a beachfront property in Miami that he stayed in to do his twice-yearly proofs. His Juneteenth proof in June and his Christmas proof in December. So there was no way to guess that coming to Big Canoe was even a tiny possibility. Unlike any other time we've had a microscope conversation, she is eerily quiet throughout this one. I look to see if the call is still connected a couple of times. Either she is wholly uninterested in what I'm saying, which would be a first, or she's so deep into analyzing it that she doesn't even have the bandwidth to speak.

"So Dillin stormed out, me and Vanny finished closing up, I texted you, and then I came home."

Just off the kitchen in our house is a little nook with a coffee table and a couple of loveseats. That's where I am now, my tea on a side table, my phone on my chest as I lay looking at the night sky through the rain-splattered glass portion of the roof above me.

"I've never been this disappointed in you, House."

She sounds angry. But she called me by my nickname. But her tone is like steel. So she's definitely mad. Well, as she said, she's disappointed, actually. I didn't invite him home, I didn't get his number, I didn't give him mine, I didn't even flirt back for fuck's sake. How many people am I going to let down today?

"I'm sorry, Tory. I really am trying. But this caught me so off guard. I mean, what are the odds that he was lying about his house in Miami and came here every year? I'm sorry, please don't be mad."

"Oh, calm down. It's fine. Well, it will be when you commit to my advice. Are you ready to do that?"

I clutch the phone and sit up.

"Well...what exactly would I be committing to?"

"Nope. Gotta commit first. No chicken shit."

I sigh. I'm lightweight terrified, but I know Tory wouldn't ask me to promise to do something too far outside my comfort zone. I hope.

"Okay. I promise," I take a sip of my tea, lukewarm now, and sit it back on the side table.

"The next time you see Reave, you have to ask him if he'll fuck you. That needs to be the first shit out of your mouth."

I stand so abruptly I almost drop the phone.

"What?!"

"You heard me. Based on what you said he's ready for it. He might be holding back because he sees how reserved you are in social situations. But if *you* tell *him* you want it? It's a done deal. You do want him, right?"

"Of course! You know how I feel about him. And you've seen what he looks like, but that's beside the point. Why would that be the first thing out of my mouth? What if he shows up at IGA and there are other customers there? Vanny? Oh shit, *Dillin*?" Horrific scenarios are playing in my mind now. There's no way that would go well. Not to mention the sheer embarrassment that would ensue if I read Reave wrong and misinterpreted what I thought I was seeing and feeling. And if he lied about where he does his final proofs, why couldn't he have lied about dating someone or even being married? He could have an entire family and no one would know since he's such a recluse as far as celebrities go.

"See, this is what I mean. Who gives a fuck about the IGA? Who cares about Dillin Fuck-Face Rankin? And, I didn't say you had to scream so the whole store could hear. If it's at IGA, just whisper it to him. He's a smart man. He'll be discreet and nod, slide you his number, done and done." *You fucking idiot* seems to be pinned to the end of that statement, even though she doesn't say it. Her voice is just that tight, that strained. She sounds so fed up. Exactly like Nurse Donova. But I need her to think this through and see how dangerous this could be. The last thing I want is to offend or upset my idol.

"I, personally, would love it if things were that simple. But do you understand my point? This could be extremely problematic under the wrong set of circumstances. I also don't know if I'll see him again while he's here. I don't know what cabin he's in, if he's even staying in Big Canoe or somewhere nearby. I don't know for sure that he'll come to the store again while I'm working or if he'll end up coming on days when I'm off."

Tory takes a deep inhale and lets it out. I think I pushed too hard. I can't help but wonder if she's about to write me off completely. Hang up and never talk to me again. My chest tightens at the thought.

"Kasa, you said you wanted this. You want to do different things and see different people and become a different person yourself. It's hard to do any of that if you freak the fuck out every time you encounter something new. If you can't put yourself out there, be vulnerable, and deal with those consequences one way or another, how are you going to be a Big City girl like you want? The kind we talked about throughout most of Mr. Granger's English classes?"

I appreciate her trying to lighten her tone. It makes my nervousness wane a bit. Should I call attention to it, or just keep talking? Will pointing it out make things worse or better?

I smile, hoping it'll transfer into my voice. "I do want to be a Big City girl like you, Tory. It's just a...bigger leap for me than it is for you, I think."

"We're both products of Pickens County. The jump was always a big one, House," Tory says in a voice that still sounds more anger-laden than I like to hear, my nickname said almost bitterly. "Small hops aren't going to get you to the places you deserve to be in this world.

For once in your life, just say 'fuck it' and jump for shit's sake!" Now the frustration is raw and clear. My best friend is overtly pissed at me.

"Tory, I'm so sorry."

She scoffs before giving me a weak "you always are" and clearing her throat. Tory gets pretty riled up when she's watching a movie with characters in it she doesn't like, or if she sees some injustice in the world on the news. But she's not generally a person who becomes visibly angry. Something has to really shove her hard in that direction. I wilt at the idea that it could be me doing the shoving. She hasn't sounded this furious since her parents divorced when we were seventeen. And even then, I knew some sort of explosion or breakdown might come because I knew the divorce might be coming. She'd overheard them considering it together. She kept me up to date on the increasingly frequent arguments, her mother working longer and longer hours, her father bringing "co-workers" to the house while her mother was out.

"A big part of why I left Big Canoe was your mom, House."

"Mom?" I don't understand what the connection could be there.

"Yes. She's just so alive and full of energy and then one day she just isn't because of some stupid disease that none of us can see or do shit about. My parents seemed happy together, the perfect example of a loving couple, then one day they just don't love each other anymore and I have to pick who I want to live with."

What she wants to say is starting to come together in my head, but I let her get it out.

"Things die quick, is all I'm saying. And you never know how many opportunities you'll get to do something. At one point, it was the last time we would all eat dinner together. At one point, it was the last time I would ever see my parents hug or kiss or cook together. And I know that taking my chances—with choosing to sit next to you in first grade, with the move to Atlanta, with fighting for Allana—has given me all of the best parts of my life. Since I love you, I want that for you. But every time you get a chance, it's like you sabotage it instead of embracing it."

The bubble of shame inside me grows. She continues after a few seconds of silence pass.

"It's just a…'tomorrow isn't promised' kind of thing. I know we're still sort of young, but time is always ticking. I really used to wonder if, when we first found out about the cancer, your mom would've been okay with dying. Not like she *wanted* to. But if she would have any regrets. Had she accomplished and experienced everything she wanted to?"

"Obviously not since she's gallivanting around Europe with Dad," I murmur and she laughs, making me feel some small relief, easing some of the tension of this heavy topic so I can stand to keep listening without breaking down myself. I can feel the threat of tears burning my sinuses. I don't want her to know just how bad her frustration is impacting me. She has every right to feel that way. Hell, I feel that way about myself sometimes.

"Right. So, sometimes when you tell me stuff like this, I get frustrated with your fear and your hesitancy. You're not being fair to yourself, House. Please just do that for me." Her voice is weaker now, and echoes Nurse Donova's tone. *Please leave*.

She's gotten it out, said what she had to say, and it took a lot out of her. I've seen this from her before. There's no fight left, just sadness. I swallow the lump in my throat.

"Okay, Tory. I'm sorry my—"

"And will you stop fucking apologizing!" she gives a short laugh of exasperation and then sighs.

"I'm...I will work on that."

It's well after midnight by the time we end the call. I don't know how she's going to make it into the office by seven in the morning, but she swears she has a system that involves a lot of caffeine and cat naps in the utility closet as needed. I let my frustration out with some tears and try to process what she told me about how she felt. I know that these past three years, she's been as happy as ever. Even through challenges and mishaps, she's bounced back from it all because she was living the life we'd always wanted to. She's the best bestie because she wants that for me. So much that it hurts her to see me not have it.

Nurse Donova obviously sees something promising in me that I hope is actually there. Something that can stagnate if I stay here. She doesn't want that for me. Approaching her seventies, I'm sure she's seen it happen too many times. Part of me suspects that she sees herself as having experienced the same thing. Talent and passion and time squandered because it's safe and comfortable here compared to new and strange challenges somewhere else. Even Vanny nudges me to go after what I want. These women all want me to be Kasa+ now. Not when I get to Atlanta, as if crossing the city limits will magically change me into a new woman.

Pajama-clad I slide under the heavy blanket on my bed. As mature and upscale as I'm trying to be, I'll never kick the habit of wearing a good onesie. This set is pure white, the zipper on the front has a pull that's shaped like a carrot, and it has a hood with long, white rabbit ears on it. The epitome of sleepwear bliss. Being bottom heavy, the material is a bit tight around the hips and stomach, but plenty comfortable for lounging around the house.

I grab my copy of *The Flavor of Magic* and continue my second reading of it. And, of course, as if there hadn't been enough signs for me today, I'm at the point in the story where the main character has to choose what to do with her newfound power. Will she hide it away to keep her city safe from the government's soldiers and let it kill her from the inside out, or will she use her power to start a revolution? Stay stagnant and temporarily safe or move bravely into the unknown and truly live? I don't have any political systems to dismantle, and I certainly don't have any magical powers. But I still have a decision to make. No, not a decision to make. Action to *take*. Anyone can have dreams or a plan or a desire. I need to take concrete steps toward what I want.

A couple of pages later, the main character's younger sister arrives at home to see her front yard blazing with orbs of light magic rolling in patterns along the ground and swirling up into the night sky. Dressed in his coronation garb, the finest clothes he owns, a prince-turned-war-criminal is prostrate in the dirt beside her front steps. He completes the engagement ritual by requesting her hand in marriage, not allowed to rise until she gives her answer.

I get to the middle of that scene, just before she gives her terrified assent, before I'm laying down with the book on my belly, staring up at the skylight in my room. My Dad's obsessed with being able to see the sky, always has been. And with him being a construction guru, there's no way we weren't going to be seeing the heavens with every step we took in this house. Even the one in my room below ground is a result of him creating a column of space within the house leading up to the roof. And I love it. Being able to feel like I am out in the open forest without the weather and wildlife. Over the years, being able to look up into the cosmos from my bed has helped me think. See things clearly. Put them in perspective. This window to the stars—along with Reave's fascinating imaginary worlds—helped a selfish little girl who just wanted to flee decide to buckle down and help her family. That it was more important to put her needs aside for the sake of the person who had brought her into this world in the first place.

But now? Now is different. This

isn't about my mother's health. Once Mom and Dad return, there is nothing standing in my way. I can leave like I've always wanted with a clear conscience. And I will. But I have to wonder if I need to completely leave Big Canoe behind just to start acting like the woman I want to be.

I put the book on the bedside table, turn out the light and take one more look at Reave on my phone. Gorgeous, brilliant, and so close today. Yet, still feeling like a million miles away. As extreme as it would be to do so, I think following through on my commitment to Tory would be good for me. Force me out of my comfort zone in a growthful way, regardless of how embarrassing it may feel in the moment.

I put my phone on its charging station and snuggle deeper under the covers. The raindrops hitting hard against the glass above me, the deep darkness of my room, and the cozy warmth of the fur-lined onesie start pulling me down into sleep within seconds. It also helps that I've made up my mind.

I promise myself that Kasa+ will be born tomorrow.

3

I'm off today. I wake up and start my morning in a familiar and anticlimactic fashion. Shower, slip into another onesie (a fox this time), text Tory a meme, make tea, read. I usually don't get hungry until around lunchtime, so the tea is enough of a "breakfast" for my body. I decide to start another book that I've been wanting to read by an author other than Reave because there's no way I'm going to be able to concentrate otherwise.

Dad calls to give me an update on the trip and it sounds like they're both having a fantastic time. I'm glad I was able to contribute in some small way by housesitting. I tell him about Reave being in town and he brings Mom to the phone so we can all three freak out about it. I leave out all the flirty stuff, of course. But they are just as excited as I am at the prospect that I might see him a few more times before I'm no longer in Big Canoe for most of the year as an Atlanta transplant.

After our call, I do a little tidying up. As I'm finishing sweeping the porch, I realize that I never brought my Santa Cheese in. I'd been too excited about talking to Tory. Sitting the broom just inside the front door, I go and grab the IGA bag, the cheese still chilled from being out in the cold all night, and make my way up the porch steps. Behind me, I can hear the sound of a car making its way past our house, headed to the last cabin on this street, meaning someone's rented it out.

Even though most of the folks in Big Canoe at any given time are permanent residents, we're the only ones on this particular road. Living around a tourist area has led to some interesting interactions, but it meant that I never got "neighbors" so to speak. Everyone who stayed only did so for a weekend, a week at the most. The massive homes and beautiful scenery are a major draw, especially when the leaves change in the fall.

Sometimes, as I was walking to meet up with Tory or taking a stroll with a new audiobook, I'd catch a set of weekenders out for a hike, or doing yoga on their patio, or saying their goodbyes in their driveways. Generally, I would just give a friendly wave. Every now and then, someone would ask me which cabin I was renting, but I'd tell them I grew up here and they'd call me lucky and a (normally) brief conversation would start. Just like reading about the characters in Reave's books, I loved getting to know these various people and getting an idea of what their everyday world must be like. I'd always compare their lives to mine and mine always lost, seeming boring and ordinary. No matter where someone told me they lived or what they said they were studying or what industry they worked in, I would be in awe of them. And yet, for them, Big Canoe looked like a getaway. A paradise, even. I started to learn then that the grass always seems greener somewhere else.

Mom used to tell me that this was

a reason to be careful about considering an "all-in" move to ATL. It might not be everything I had it cracked up to be. But it wasn't like I hadn't been to Atlanta dozens of times. From family outings to school trips, the city was all too familiar to me. It was hard for there to be any real misconception about what it was like. And now that Tory had been living there for three years, she was fully immersed in it as an Atlanta resident. And I got all the nitty gritty details direct from the horse's mouth. If I wasn't scared of, or tired of, Atlanta by now, there was little chance that I would be any time in the near future. Even as Tory regularly shares the increasingly criminal prices of housing, groceries, and gas down there, it doesn't deter me a bit.

When I reenter the house and close the door behind me, I get as far as the laundry room around the corner on the upper level before there's a knock on the front door. I put the broom back where it belongs as I try to think of the last time I ordered a package, but I don't have anything on the way. Tory's in Atlanta, my parents are still in Europe.

The only two people I know of who

know where I live and would have any reason to visit me at home are Dillin and Vanny. But neither of them would come up the mountain after me. Vanny would just wait until my next shift or call me if she had something to tell me. I suppose Dillin could be childish enough to still be mad about Reave's comment last night, but not enough to show up on my doorstep.

Curious, I open the Ring app on my phone to see who's waiting outside.

It's Reave.

My gut is in my toes and my heart starts practically vibrating it's beating so fast. He fidgets in dark jeans and a black button-down shirt, his locs loose around his face. What the hell is he doing at my house? Could Vanny have told him where I live? No, he hadn't come back to the store last night, so there's no way she could have told him. If he only comes in near closing, then he wouldn't be back until tonight. He'd have no reason to go back to IGA yet.

Except for the Santa Cheese.

Being the honorable person he is, he probably realized what had happened and gone back to IGA to pay for the cheese. Then Vanny could have told him. Or maybe another manager? Would he have asked—

"Hello?" Reave's voice comes through the door with another set of three knocks. I put my phone in one of the giant pockets of my onesie and wince. Why am I never in my regular clothes when he's around? I consider changing, but don't want to risk him thinking no one's home and leaving. My spine straightens as I convince myself that Kasa+ changes for no man. Kasa+ is sexy in everything she wears.

Instead of further speculating, I walk to back to the landing, resolving to just ask him how he got my address and why in the world he's stalking me like some crazed fan. No big deal.

But the second I open the front door and see the way he looks at me—like I'm the meal he's been waiting days to eat—all I can think of is my promise to Tory. Well, that and the fact that I have no sensible out. We aren't at the IGA or in public at all. We are right here on my porch, private property, at the end of a street, tucked away from any prying eyes or ears. What excuse do I have to *not* do what I said I would?

"Hey. Kasa," he says, his voice suiting my name all too well, causing me to press my thighs a little tighter together. Especially when I think about the fact that he could very well say "yes." He could accept my offer and within minutes we'd be in my bed. I roll my lips into my mouth and bite down hard on them. I refuse to whimper in front of him just yet.

"I just wanted to thank you for the cheese. I brought you some," he says, holding up an IGA bag I hadn't noticed yet. "They got some more in stock. I went back to the store and paid for the one you gave me. I kinda felt guilty." He chuckles and rubs his hand across his mouth nervously before his stunning eyes find mine again. "I saw you out here on the porch on my way back and I thought it's kind of a coincidence that I'm renting the cabin right next to yours. Just thought I'd say it in person. Thank you, I mean. Not the coincidence thing. Though, I did to that, I guess."

He's adorably anxious and finally pauses to take a breath. Here goes nothing.

"Will you have sex with me?"

I say it on an exhale and now I feel like I'll never fill my own lungs again. How did those edgy, sophisticated women we saw online do this day-to-day? I feel like I'm about to melt in the cool autumn air, right here on my porch with Reave watching.

His silence is unsettling, but the way his eyes trail up and down my body again give me confidence that I didn't just royally embarrass myself. If he can look at me like that in my IGA vest and messy bun and in my comfy fox pajamas, I can't possibly be misinterpreting what he wants. He reestablishes his grip on the grocery bag of Santa Cheese as it almost slips from his fingers. Him being as thrown off as I feel helps ease my anxiety a little.

"I...uh...I would love nothing more."

I immediately step back into the house and motion for him to enter, nothing but a shrieking stream of OH MY GOD WHAT THE FUCK DID YOU JUST DO ARE YOU REALLY GOING TO SLEEP WITH REAVE FUCKING ALAMI WHAT THE FUCK IS WRONG WITH YOU on a loop in my head. The same loop that makes me stop when I think I'm being aggressive or demanding. When I think I'm asking too much of someone, even if part of me knows it's just my due, nothing more and nothing less. I let the words crowd my mind, but stay my course. Just because they are cycling through my brain doesn't mean I have to let them deter me. I get to choose my actions, even when my mind is going haywire.

I take the bag from him as I thank him and then head up to the kitchen to put it in the fridge. I hear him take off his shoes on the landing and close the front door. I hold the refrigerator door open longer than necessary, trying to chill the heat that seems to have sprung up all over my body like some kind of rash. When I finally close it, he's in the kitchen entry about ten feet away, looking at me with curiosity and lust. Hunger, even. It's like he's restraining himself from doing... what, exactly? Maybe he's still processing what I said. Wondering if I really meant it. Wanting clearer consent before he tells me what he wants. Dillin never gives that much pause. But that's no surprise since Reave is everything that Dillin isn't. And everything I want.

"So...what did you have in mind?" he asks.

What *don't* I have in mind when it comes to fucking him?

I kind of want to say that out loud, but Basic Kasa is fighting hard. Basic Kasa wants me to kick him out, quit the IGA, abandon the house for the month so he can't find me again, and pretend none of this mortifying past 24 hours' ever happened. But Kasa+ will prevail. Somehow. When she figures out which of her fantasies she wants to play out. After all, this may be my only chance. Sexy scenes from my imagination are flickering through my head. I'm not sure if I'll ever choose or if I'll be paralyzed with indecision to the point that he gets exasperated and walks out.

"This is so much easier when someone tells me what to do." *That?* That's what I say out loud? Perfect.

Reave's eyes narrow and he takes a step toward me, still keeping what I figure he thinks is a respectful distance away. I must look like such a scared little bunny to him, foxy onesie or no. But it complements the air of a wolf that he's bringing to the table. I love the way he looks like he wants to…well…*reave* me.

"You don't know what you want?" he asks.

I shake my head. "I do. I really do. This is just…different for me."

Understatement of the year.

"That's fairly obvious," he reaches for my face, takes another step with his long legs, and pulls me into a kiss. Just a tap of the lips, but it has my mouth watering.

"I have an idea," he continues, then kisses me again, this time tracing the line between my lips with his tongue. I part them to give him access to my mouth, but he pulls away again, leaving me panting and aching. I've got it much worse for him than I thought if this is all it takes to get me this excited. On my end, at least, this is it. He is The One for me.

"Kasa," he whispers, sliding down to his knees in front of me. The sight of his eager eyes looking up at me as he grips my ass means I won't be able to stand on my own much longer. "I demand that you command me."

Damn.

Even my breaths are shaky now, his

touch stinging me through the fur-lined fleece I'm wearing. The vision of him kneeling before me like this is making it hard to think. But I remind myself that I don't have to think. Technically, he told me what to do. He opened the door. He told me to command him. To say what I want.

He told me to be Kasa+ *right now*.

As I've wanted to do since I ran into him at IGA, I plunge my hand into his hair, the tendrils cool and sleek in my fingers. His eyes slide closed like he's in sheer ecstasy at my touch. He gives a short moan and leans backward into my palm. The sound is like a tremor working its way from my knees and up my spine, making me release the whimper I've been fighting to hold back.

I'm not gonna make it to the bedroom.

"You...carry me."

He immediately stands and lifts me, pulling my thighs around his waist. He's massaging my ass as I wrap myself tighter around him. He kisses beside my mouth and I chase his lips with my own, but he pulls back again, cocking an eyebrow.

"I'm sorry. What was that?" he purrs,

tilting an ear toward me as if I'd actually said something and he'd actually missed it.

I let out a giggle.

"Kiss me, Reave," I order.

His name leaves my mouth as his tongue enters it. I tell myself that refraining from having him fuck me right here on the counter is not me being too restrained. It's just me wanting to prolong this a little more. To enjoy this wet dream come true.

I put a finger over his lips during one of the half-seconds when his mouth separates from mine.

"Take me downstairs to the bedroom," I get out in a rush, wanting his tongue back inside me as soon as possible. Just as I'm about to pull my hand away, he takes my index finger in his mouth and swirls his tongue around it in a dizzying motion as he begins walking through the living space.

"Fuck," I breathe, having to close my eyes against the vision of me being in his mouth. I feel him angle around the dining room table and step carefully down to the landing where the front door is, turn and finish the descent to the lower level.

At the bottom of the stairs, we stop moving, and so does his tongue.

"Reave!" I whine and watch in wonder as his eyes slam shut and he groans with my finger in his feverish mouth. Now he's got me curious about what else I can do to make him weak. Parting his lips, he clamps my fingernail between his teeth, asking "'ich wan?" I nod toward my room, the door closest to the stairs. He turns right and vacuums me back into his mouth. The reentry heats every part of me all over again. He gently lays me down on my unmade bed, looking down at me expectantly. A dutiful knight awaiting direction from his queen.

"Just let me watch you. Like this. Just for a minute," I know this is probably awkward for him, but if I'm being honest about what I want, this is it. My favorite author, the man I fell in love with from a thousand stories away, is in my room, in my bed, ready to please me in whatever way I ask him to. I'm confident that what comes after this moment will be amazing, and I do want to get to that part. But having him hovering over me with his lithe arms and wide mouth, hair that I mussed and eyes that at least give the impression that he *has* to have me, is too good to be true. I just want to douse myself in it—his gaze, his scent, his warmth—for a few more beats.

Even though there's a pulse of concern between his eyebrows for a second, he lets me. And the way he looks at me, as if telling me, *showing me*, that this is real and mine and I deserve this almost brings me to relieved tears. But when he shifts from holding himself on his hands to supporting himself on his elbows, his denim-clad erection rubs against my thigh and I know it's time to make a move.

I clear my throat.

"Stand up and take off your clothes," I say, still feeling a little nervous about the directness. But he's eating it up, giving me confidence.

He dips down to sear me with another kiss before crawling backwards off of the bed and obeying me. His lips are little rewards for saying what I want, I'm starting to realize. He trails his fingers across my body as he goes, like he's trying his hardest to soak my onesie through my underwear. Once he's standing, he starts with the button-down. I'm torn between telling him to slow down and speed up, so I just let him go at his own pace and let my eyes feast on him.

The shirt comes off and lands on the floor, a white tee underneath. His arms are lean, flexing as he peels off the tee and starts on his pants. He moves more carefully, protecting the sensitive protrusion as he lets his jeans and boxers down simultaneously, revealing his long, toned legs and delectable-looking erection in a single motion.

As soon as he kicks the garments aside, I start scrambling to get out of my pajamas, standing and tearing the front zipper down my body.

"Kasa," he says and I freeze. "Please?" he asks, walking up to me and reaching for the zipper, but not touching it. He wants to undress me. It's sweet and sexy and only increases the anticipation, so I nod and let my hand fall away from the zipper that hasn't quite made it over my breasts yet. I swear he can see my stiff nipples through the fur and the fleece since I'm not wearing a bra, but it could be my imagination.

He bends to plunge into my mouth

again, one hand going to the back of my head. He taps my giant hair clip twice, backs away and arches an eyebrow at me. I nod again and he opens the clip, letting my hair fall across my shoulders. He wraps his hand in it and kisses me again as he continues pulling my zipper down.

When he pulls his lips away, I'm about two seconds from collapsing backwards onto the bed. Every time he kisses me I wish it would last forever. He takes his long fingers to my shoulders and slowly pushes the sides of my pajamas down. Making as much contact with my skin as possible as the sleeves fall and then crouches in front of me once again, pulling the rest of my onesie down to the floor. He gently kisses my belly button and then takes an obscenely deep inhale with his nose wedged between my legs. Now they do give out and I sit on the bed.

He laughs as he starts pulling off my panties. "Sorry about that. Couldn't help myself."

I bounce on the bed to allow him to pull the fabric under my hips and past my thighs. He grazes the back of my knees and calves, then pulls my underwear past my feet and tosses them aside, his eyes never leaving mine.

I put a hand to the side of his face, rubbing a thumb over his lips. I've always found him attractive, but seeing him in photographs and on YouTube videos can't hold a candle to him in person.

He leans his cheek into my palm and turns to kiss it as I give voice to my next desire. I'm not on birth control and I'm relatively certain he didn't plan for any of this to happen to the point that he would have condoms on him. Even though that cut my fantasy selection by about two-thirds, I still have a lot of options. I select one.

"I want to sit on your face now," I tell him. He grins, his eyes light up, and I have to close my eyes again so I don't get overwhelmed. At this point, he could probably just breathe on my clit and I'd be done for. I spin around and get on all fours, ass facing the head of the bed. He comes around to the foot of the bed, bends down to kiss me, making me laugh. Then he slides backwards between my arms and legs until his head is under my ass and his dick is nearly taking my eye out, the wide head glistening with pre-cum. I feel saliva filling my mouth, but I just let it fall. I'll need it anyway. He's inhaling me again and the sound sends electricity up my spine. He grabs my hips, pulling me down on him. I'm not a small girl, so part of me is afraid of suffocating him. I'm not fond of the idea of being responsible for the death of a celebrity, especially not in a circumstance like this. But I trust him to tell me if it's too much.

I lightly settle back, feeling like I'm sitting on a motorcycle. The feel of his warm breath against my labia and continuing to feel him claw at me as if I'm not sitting down hard enough already has my heart racing like I'm headed toward a climax. I brace myself mentally as I do as his body asks and relax, spreading my knees a few inches wider, putting all 220 pounds of my body onto his skull.

He whimpers and I feel it all over my skin. He smacks my ass before turning his focus to my clit and not letting up for a second. I do my best to concentrate, grabbing for his dick, only able to get the first inch or so into my mouth from this angle since he's so much taller than me. This gives me new respect for the actresses online who make this look so effortless. How do you keep your brain functioning at all when someone is eating you out like the fate of the world depends on it?

A piece of me wants to tell him to wait or slow down. But this feels too damn good. I didn't realize it could be this phenomenal to have someone between my legs like this. I knew Dillin had to be a dud, but I figured Tory may have been exaggerating about some of her nights with Allana. I owe her a massive apology.

Reave's tongue seems impossibly long, hot, and wet. His nose is practically up my asshole, but he legitimately doesn't seem to care. Something about knowing he's enjoying himself magnifies the effect of every lash of his tongue. Even the cool intake of air I feel when he pulls away to take a breath arouses me as it shocks the skin of my pussy. Between moans, I try my best to lick and suck him, fondling his balls as I've done with Dillin before. Being able to play this out with someone I am attracted to is an invigorating feeling. So much so that I realize I'm close to the edge. Pleasure pools between my thighs in preparation for the internal fireworks.

"Shit...Reave...I'm there...Just keep..."

And I'm gone.

Sitting up straight, his tongue piercing me, and every nerve ending in my body singing his praises, my ass bounces on his forehead as I quiver and shout his name. My fingernails dig into his forearms as they wrap around me while he caresses my nipples like he reveres them, as if they are the most precious things on Earth. My vision fills with bright stars and my spine lights up like a power line. As I'm coming down, trying to lean forward to suck him again, he holds my biceps in fingers like iron and forces me harder onto his face and in a matter of seconds there's another monsoon of euphoria crashing over me. I'm glad he's holding me in place because I can hardly feel any part of my body beyond my clit, let alone balance on top of him very well. After the second one, he finally lets me go. I slide forward hearing a sound like someone stirring pasta as my wet skin separates from his face. The sound of Reave panting follows soon after. I crawl back down to my post, grazing his balls with my fingers again and rubbing the base of my tongue in a circle on one side of his head.

Beneath me, Reave's squirming, his breath getting even faster, ragged. Short bursts of sounds escape him and I feel him pulling on the sheets.

So fucking hot.

Though I've never been a fan of Dillin's cum, Reave will be different. Maybe the taste will be similar, but the fact that it belongs to Reave, in my mind, makes all the difference. I want any and every part of him I can get. For this, I don't have to wait. I don't have to put what I want on the back burner. I can take what I crave without guilt or shame herding my actions.

I cup his nuts with one hand and stroke with the other as I turn to speak over my shoulder.

"Come for me right now, Reave. I wanna taste you." I immediately put him back in my mouth, not sure how long he'll last after that. My jaw barely closes around him in time.

There's no sweeter sound than him groaning my name, bucking against me, his toes curling and heels digging into the mattress as hot creaminess spurts into my mouth in waves.

I drink it down without hesitation. The taste barely registers since his tip is on the back of my tongue, there's just liquid warmth and a little saltiness.

This is *nothing* like the old me.

It's filthy.

It's glorious.

4

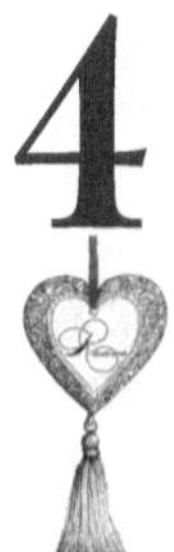

After draining Reave, I roll off of him and take a minute to calm myself. Both of us are sprawled on my bed like we just ran a marathon and collapsed at the finish line. What I wouldn't give for another day like this. Then again, he'll be here all month long. But he'll have work to do. He'll need to take breaks, though, right? But I want him to hurry up and finish because he's probably working on the sequel to *Sanarada*. The first book was a wild ride, so I'm excited to see where the heroine, Zin, will go next now that's she's saved the Sanaradan village filled with disabled orcs and found her true love, Meron. I'd like to think I've found my Meron, but I'm sure he doesn't feel the same. Who falls for someone after the first time they have sex? After meeting less than 24 hours ago? After dreaming about being with them for a decade?

After creating a fan club for them for shit's sake?

I don't realize I've dozed off until Reave's lips are on mine again.

I open my eyes and see him smiling down at me. I can smell and taste myself on him, still see some moisture on his face from my arousal, and it makes me grin.

"My beautiful Meron," I say, only meaning to think it, but my brain is too buoyant, still riding the fumes of pleasure.

Reave looks confused and then concerned.

"Who?"

"Meron," I laugh. "You created him and now you don't know who he is?"

Reave crawls off of me like I just burst into flame. I sit up too fast, making myself dizzy.

"What is it?" I ask, following him with my eyes as he collects his clothes and starts putting them back on.

What the fuck?

"I should've known better, that's what," he growls, ripping his tee over his head then jamming his feet down into his boxers.

There's ice in the pit of my stomach now.

"A...bout...what?" Is he really having regrets this quickly? Nothing in his body language or his words over the course of the past half hour have signified that he didn't want this as much as I did. Or that he wasn't enjoying himself. What the hell changed that quick?

I pull the comforter up over my breasts.

"You didn't even ask me my name. You *knew* it already. How could I be so fucking stupid?" he put his legs into his jeans with more sharp, harsh movements. "I gave you the benefit of the doubt. I thought maybe you saw it on the receipt from my credit card or something. But I never told you my name. And you didn't look at the receipt, now that I think about it. You snatched it out of the machine and handed it to me already folded. Even if my name was printed on it you wouldn't have seen it. You didn't look at my card because I never gave it to you. Stupid, stupid, fucking stupid!" he roars.

"I don't understand—" I start to say, voice thickening with tears, but he cuts me off.

"I know. I know you don't get it. I shouldn't expect you to. Just—" he puts a fist to his lips, composing himself for a beat. "Thank you. This was...thank you. Have a good day." Button-down in hand, he turns and bolts. I hear him struggling with his shoes when he gets to the landing, and then the front door slams behind him.

I'm sitting on my bed after having just had sex with my dream guy, someone I've idolized since I was a child, and I have no idea how things went so wrong so quickly.

I breathe in and I can still smell his cologne. He *was* here. I look down and see the spot drenched with my saliva where I drank him in. He *was* here. It had happened. It wasn't a hallucination, or a dream. Reave Alami had been here and he had fucked me, and we had enjoyed ourselves.

But something about mentioning Meron spooked him. Bad.

I get up, tears burning in my eyes, and fish in my pajama pockets for my phone. I text a microscope, broken heart, and teary face to Tory and then run through the events that just took place in my head over and over again until she calls.

I lay the situation out to her. Still feeling as if it happened to someone else. But I won't deny the pleasurable part of this day, so I have to take this bizarre turn along with it.

"Okay. So, obviously it has something to do with the book. If this Meron person isn't a villain of some kind..." I can hear clicking. She doesn't wear that many cowry shells in her hair, so if I'm hearing them hit each other, she's tying herself up in knots. "Why would you comparing him to one of his own characters be a bad thing? Not just bad, but offensive enough for him to storm out?"

"I don't know," I say. Then add, as the thought occurs to me, "I can't...go to Atlanta."

"What?" Tory coughs as if something she was drinking went down wrong.

"I can't, Tory. This is my first Kasa+ experience and look how bad I fucked it up. Moving to Atlanta would just be one catastrophe after another. I'd probably find a way to ruin your life too and I couldn't be responsible for that."

"Kasa, stop it. Based on what you

told me, everything did go great. You spoke up. You told him what you wanted and he gave it to you. That's it. This thing at the end is just a fluke. Nothing in life is perfect, there's no such thing. Today was amazing with a bit of weirdness at the end, that's all. And remember that we can fix this."

"Fix it?"

"Yes. You're an adult. Go talk to him. Ask him what happened. Apologize if you need to, but don't let it end like this."

"Even if that were going to work, how would I do that? I don't have his number or his email address. I could try to contact him through his website, but his webmaster is handling that and I'm sure he doesn't want this shared with other people. If I walk over there, he's not going to let me in."

"And that doesn't sound like self-sabotage to you?"

I run a hand through my unbound hair in frustration. Unfortunately, that just reminds me of why it's down in the first place, of Reave's mouth and hands on me. Tory continues.

"Honestly, I love the whole 'Kasa+' name. That's a good way to look at your transformation. But you need to *be* her. Now, not later. Atlanta or Big Canoe or Savannah, she needs to exist. Kasa+ would already be on her way to Reave's cabin, regardless of what his reaction is going to be. If he's going to be your next man or your ex fling, at least go find out."

I lay back on the bed, hyper aware of the smell of him on the pillows.

"Thanks," I say, not really focused on her, my mind still processing what could have gone wrong.

Wait. Ex?

"Oh...son of a bitch." I sit up, the phone sliding from my fingers. "Karen goddamn Williams. I'm such an idiot." I bury my face in my hands.

"Am I allowed to know what this sudden breakthrough is?" Tory's voice is muffled since my phone ended up under my thigh somehow.

"Tory...I'm an idiot. I just...as far I we know, Reave has only ever had one girlfriend. Karen Williams, some journalist for NeoNewz."

"Okay, I'm following."

"This was about five years ago. He and she both kept things about their breakup pretty quiet, but there was a lot of speculation and a lot of circumstantial evidence, as you would call it, pointing to the breakup being caused by her using him."

"How do you use an author? Well, other than what you did today. Still proud of you for that, BTdub."

I roll my eyes, swallow the rising lust at the memory of my body on his, and continue.

"Well, *she* was using him to advance her career. Whenever he had a new book coming out, she would sneak into his Docs account and get excerpts from it so she could tease it on her professional blog. People knew she had an in with him and would request exclusives and private details to try to sell more ads on their online content. Once they went public with their relationship, she became even more of a hot commodity. The last straw was her leaking the first *Sanarada* book. It wasn't supposed to come out until February and she leaked it in December when he would have been doing his Christmas proof like he does every year."

"I bet his fans ate that up. But did they know it was unauthorized?"

"No, we didn't. We thought it was a

treat he was giving to his fans and just releasing it through her because they were a couple. She even said so on the post that had the book attached as a PDF. She said it was his Christmas present to us. She had an obscene amount of activity on that post. Still does now that it's so controversial, now that everyone knows that she didn't really have permission to do that. Well, now that we suspect that anyway."

"He still hasn't confirmed that she did it maliciously? Or at least without permission?" Her shells click together again. She'll pull her plaits out of her head at this rate.

"Never. That's why everything is so up in the air regarding facts versus speculation. But, Tory, if that's true, then of course he fled the moment I mentioned one of his character's names. And in December no less! During his Christmas proof. He must think that I'm some fan just trying to use the encounter to get some kind of traffic boost online or to sell an exclusive story. God, how humiliating. And I'm so ashamed that he might think that about me."

"No no no! No wallowing and no

pity. What I said still stands. This is fixable. Go and talk to him. Right now. Well, assuming you're appropriately clothed again."

I get off the phone so I can go and do just that. But when I make my way down the road to the last house, there's no car in the wooden car port big enough for four. I walk up to the door and knock, calling out for him. But there's no answer and I don't see or hear any movement from inside. I walk around the side to check the patio, just to be sure. He must have driven off right after he got back.

For the entire rest of the day, I have my ears perked up, listening for the sound of a car passing my house. I snack on the highest-calorie things I can find in the kitchen, food always my go-to for comfort when I'm feeling stressed. A little chocolate here, a little cheese there—not the Santa Cheese, though, I can't bring myself to touch that yet—and my anxiety about the situation starts to decrease by a tiny bit. Three more times I go over to the house just to make sure I didn't miss his return. This goes on for the rest of the night. The last time, after grabbing one of Dad's grease pencils, I walk over to his house at a frigid one a.m. All signs point to him not coming back before dawn.

On the porch, right in front of the door, I write "KAsa TAnaka CRUz." The end of the 'z' is stunted because, in only a light jacket, I'm trembling on the freezing planks and rush to stand and run back home. I don't know if revealing my identity will help or hurt what's going on between us, but it's all I have that might make him understand that I mean him no harm. No. That I *love* him.

More tears come as I make my way back.

He has to come back at some point. He wouldn't abandon a month-long rental two days in. Then again, he probably could afford to. And if I'd really reminded him of his ex to that degree, maybe he was traumatized enough that he would just go back home to Louisville and never return to Big Canoe again.

How can I have fucked this up so bad?

Reave doesn't appear at IGA for the next six days. Even when I'm off, I ride down to hang out in the parking lot, waiting for him to show up. I've gone into complete creep mode.

Whenever I go to his cabin, even when I see his car in the car port, he doesn't answer the door. Each visit, I limit myself to knocking and asking to be let in three times before I walk away. I don't want to bug him when he's working on what will be my next favorite piece from him. And even though I understand that this may have been more of a one-time encounter, I don't want it to end this way. With tension and pain between us. To add insult to injury, masturbating now pales in comparison to what we've done. Dillin never put a tenth of that much effort into pleasing me. Hell, even considering that I could be pleased. He just didn't care. But Reave *needed* me to come on his face. His pleasure was intertwined with my own, and I felt the same, and that added an element to the orgasm that can't be substituted.

"Hey, Fingers. Why don't we take a little trip to the stock room?" Dillin asks, nodding toward the back of the store and already walking in front of me right after I clock in the following Friday night. It's the first time since the night Reave came in that he's asked me. There's no way I can do it. Not after being with Reave. Reave and I aren't a couple either, but things between us feel both too intimate and too unresolved for me to do anything even remotely sexual with Dillin. This is in addition to the fact that nothing I'd ever done with Dillin could measure up to that single half-hour with Reave. I used to go along to get along, but Reave has shown me better. Shown me what sex with a loving, respectful partner who craves my pleasure is like. I'll never settle for anything less again.

So I turn in the opposite direction, walk to the breakroom, and open my locker. Dillin comes in a few seconds behind me.

"I guess you didn't hear me. I said—"

"I heard you," I say, putting my wallet, keys, and coat in the locker and shutting it. I pat my pocket to make sure I have my phone, check that my new name badge's pin is secure, and excuse myself as I step around him and head toward the breakroom door. Dillin grabs my wrist to stop me. To my surprise, it takes everything in me not to swing at him. Some of the rage I'd felt at how he'd spoken to Reave last week is still simmering somewhere inside me, apparently. Dillin had been my first sexual partner and it irks me that he seems to still have some kind of sense of entitlement or ownership when it comes to me. But I'm not his wife or his girlfriend. I'm not even really his fuck buddy. I'm just a set of fingers that aren't his own. Nothing more. Fuck that.

"You heard me?" he asks. "So why didn't you follow me?"

"Because I don't want you."

In the back of my mind, that seems harsh. I could've said I'm not feeling well or I hurt my hand or that Vanny asked me to do something at the beginning of my shift and I couldn't ignore her instructions. I could even have said I don't want to give him a hand job or have any kind of sex with him at all. But Kasa+ took over and got straight to the heart of the matter. I do not want Dillin Rankin. Never did.

Dillin looks confused, but more like I've spoken a foreign language to him. Not like he's heard something he didn't want to hear. And how can I blame him? I have never refused him before, so this is startling territory for the both of us, really. Yet, I feel more relief than anxiety.

"You don't...want...me," he repeats, his eyes narrowing and mouth constricting like he's wondering if I'm playing some kind of joke. "So I guess you want Gramps from last week instead? You gonna wait for him to want you? Hell, to give you the time of day?"

"I fucked him this weekend. So, he's given me much more than the time." I slide my wrist out of his fist, watching his face darken with blood and his mouth turn down. I leave him standing there while I go start my shift. Either he will believe me and leave me alone or he won't. I don't mind repeating myself just to make sure he gets the message. But if he pushes, I'll go to Vanny.

The woman who would have compromised just to keep things cordial between us is gone. She'd gotten one last breath of life as I sat on my bed last week, naked, satiated, and bewildered in the wake of Reave's mad dash from my house. In that moment, I was fully ready to turn back into my old self since the Kasa+ life was clearly not for me.

But now that I understand where things went wrong, I realize that Tory is right. This is fixable. Something I can fight for. And I will. For as long and as hard as I have to for the sake of what could be between me and Reave. I won't give up until he tells me to my face that he just doesn't want me. That it has nothing to do with what I'd said and nothing to do with the ghost of Karen Williams. Only then will I try to force myself to move on. If that is even possible when I'm quite literally his biggest fan *and* crazy in love with him. I may have been open to something temporary before. But trying to go back to life without him, I see I don't really want that. I need Reave to be part of all the rest of my days.

Dillin doesn't ask again, but narrows his eyes at me all throughout the shift. I'm sure he's partly angry because he knows my refusal has to do with Reave. But he probably also thinks there's something wrong with me in general. That something happened to flip a switch in my brain so I now realize I deserve better than anything he can offer. Reave left me with that much at least.

By the end of the shift, I become aware of the fact that I haven't heard from Scammereave all week long. Being ghosted by a scammer is an extreme low. While Dillin is in the back dealing with the bailer, I end up spilling my guts to Vanny as I'm sanitizing the check lanes. Tears are barely held at bay. She's a little surprised and looks confused at first because I just start out of the blue with "I fucked Reave last week" and keep rambling from there until I get it all out.

"Well...that's certainly an adjustment from how you handled things last Friday," Vanny says after I'm quiet for a moment. She puts a fresh bag in the last small register garbage can and stands up, stretching her back as she rises.

"I know. And that's good, I guess. But now he's ghosting me, I've pissed off Dillin, and not even my scammer contacts me any more."

Vanny looks at me with a smile that has a touch of pity to it, but there's something else more positive in her expression. Maybe, like Tory, she's proud of my attempt even though it was a gargantuan fail.

"My near-elderly Vietnamese wisdom says you simply need to go home, Kasa." She smiles even wider now before walking over to the pharmacy and unlocking the display case in front of it. She pulls out a box of condoms and hands it to me. What's up with her?

"Home? Am I fired or something? And what are these? Expired?" Getting fired would be par for the course based on the week I'm having.

Hearty laughter bubbles up from her small frame. She takes the box out of my hand and puts it in my vest pocket.

"No, Kasa. You're not fired. We've had a lot of drone sales today." She approaches me and reaches up to pat my shoulder. "I really, *really* think you should just head on home now. Dillin and I will finish up. Go on."

Under pre-meeting-Reave circumstances, I might have protested. But I can't resist the hope that I'll get back home and go to his cabin and he'll actually let me in and we'll be able to work this out. Hell, if things go the way I want them to, I might even get to use the condoms Vanny's decided to gift me tonight. I hug her hard. Just like I did last Friday before all this glorious nonsense happened. I grab my stuff from the break room, sprinting past Dillin whining about having to stay a few minutes later to close up and Vanny blatantly ignoring him as she walks toward her office.

This trip up the mountain, I am determined to have it out with Reave. If I have to sleep on his front porch, that's what I'll do. I don't care how it looks or if I catch a cold, or if a bear comes and mauls me to death. I have to try. For him. For us. For myself.

I'm making a list of supplies in my head—thermoses of tea, sleeping bag, cookies, the condoms—when I see a spark of light in the trees just a few dozen feet before I get to my driveway, making me ease off the gas and slow down. It's a lazy, pulsing glow, so it's not some distant plane or light from a far-off house. If it weren't early December, I'd say it was a lightning bug.

"Maybe I'm just finally losing my fucking mind," I mumble to myself as I put my foot back on the accelerator to quickly pull into my dark driveway.

Too dark.

I usually leave the porch light on, so either the bulb's gone out or the power is off for some reason. I pull into the car port and lay my forehead on the steering wheel. This isn't by any means the worst thing that has happened recently, but it's exhausting precisely *because* it's so small. Really? *This* on top of everything else?

Reminding myself that I have much more important things to worry about than a blown bulb, I huff out a breath and get out of the car. As I turn toward the house, I see a shadow moving across the paved area in front of the porch, just visible against the night-drenched brown of the house's log face. I freeze. I can't tell what kind of animal it is, though it's long and slender. I've never heard of any kind of big cats in this area, so it doesn't seem like it could be a mountain lion. Something smaller. A bobcat, maybe?

Though I'm hoping whatever it is will slink away and allow me to safely get into the house, it just settles on the ground right in front of my steps. I try to relax and let my eyes adjust to the darkness so I can see better. But a few seconds later I'm surrounded by light.

The same kind of light I saw before I turned into the driveway.

Except, there are dozens of them, all over the place. Floating across my porch, swirling around the lone tree in the center of the small roundabout in front of the house, zooming along the black ground. I step forward so that I'm no longer under the roof of the car port and it's almost hard to tell what's a star and what isn't. The sparks have a smooth, gliding motion as they flit through the night and are more golden than white. This looks like someone bought every single lightning bug drone from IGA that they could find.

Then I realize what's happening. And my chest feels like it's filling up with lava.

I whip my head toward the shadow in front of the steps, but it's not really a shadow any more. The light has made it clear that this is the large and lithe love of my life, Reave Alami, in his black, wool long coat, prostrate on the ground before me. Just like the engagement ritual in *The Flavor of Magic.*

"Kasa Tanaka Cruz, I, Reave Mahali Alami, implore you to do me the everlasting honor of pleasing the goddesses of love and forgiving me for my behavior and distance this past week. Will you bless me this way?"

His words are slightly muffled since he's essentially speaking into asphalt and dead leaves instead of up at me. He was supposed to end the sentence by asking for an eternal bond with me in this world and the next. But I guess that would be moving a touch too fast for people who have only been within ten feet of each other three times.

Just like when he agreed to have sex with me, I pause. I take a moment to soak up the scene, my relief that he's here and speaking to me, that he did all this for me, that we have a chance to put things back the way they were between us.

Then I run to him.

"Yes!" I shout, getting to my knees and pulling him to me, kissing every part of his face I can get my lips on. I can feel him smiling as his mouth meets mine and he leans into me until I'm on my back. Shining drones dancing around us, leaves crunching under our bodies, another chance to get this right melding us together. It doesn't take long before we're both breathless and I can feel him getting hard on top of me. The sound of him groaning and whispering how much he missed me and how sorry he is are driving me almost as crazy as the taste of him and his solid warmth between my thighs.

A rustling in the trees near the house makes us both freeze. Reave sits up and looks around.

"Come on. We don't need an audience. Human, squirrel, or otherwise," he grins and offers me his hand. But when I take it, he hefts me into his arms, once again wrapping my legs around his waist. He walks me to the door, stopping to take the porch light bulb out of his pocket and screw it back in while I cling to him and giggle. He backs up to the door and laughs as I slide my key under his arm and into the lock.

Still holding me, he backs onto the landing, kicks the door closed, and finally sits me down. We get out of our shoes and hang our coats on the hooks behind the door. He smiles at me and nods toward my bedroom.

"To *talk* first, yes," I say, pulling on my cabin socks.

He holds up his palms and shrugs, with a "Fair enough" before leading me down the steps.

We lay down on the bed and I prop my head up on an arm, looking at him as he stares up at my skylight. After a few seconds, he turns his face to mine, raising his eyebrows.

"I can understand how I may have scared you. But to be next door to me for a week and not reach out...that was a lot for me."

His brow furrows and he looks ashamed, making my gut wrench.

"I'm sorry. I know you aren't like Karen."

"Really?" If he knew, why did he ghost me?

"I knew precisely because you chose Meron. That's something Karen would never have done. Would never have been able to do. She never read any of my books."

My lip curls before I can stop myself and he laughs.

"How I ended up with her is a long story, but trust me when I say I feel the same way you do about her." A wave of pain crosses over the rich brown of his beautiful face and I want nothing more than to make it go away.

"So why, Reave? If you knew then, why has it been a week since I heard from you?"

He brings his hand into the inches of space between us, splaying his fingers over the black comforter printed with various colors and sizes of cartoon paperbacks, hardcovers, and e-readers. I put my own on top of his.

"Precisely because I thought I knew, if that makes sense." He shrugs the shoulder he's not laying on. "I *knew* that Karen was the one for me. I *knew* that she was a good person. I fell for her too hard and too fast because I felt in my bones that my first impression of her was the correct one. That I hadn't missed or misinterpreted anything. That I knew everything I needed to about her and what kind of person she was."

I shake my head slightly, not wanting to interrupt, but unable to hide how perplexed I am about what he's saying. He looks down at our hands for a few seconds before continuing.

"When you called me Meron, my alarm bells went off. 'Fuck, it's happening again,' I thought. A piece of me considered the fact that you named one of my characters, meaning you did actually read my work, understand it. To the point that certain moments make you think of my characters. But then the anxiety says that's just manipulation. A way to draw me in."

I nod. Now I get it.

"So I ignored that part, did what I thought I needed to do to protect myself. My heart. As you may be able to tell by my work, I'm a bit of a romantic, so… things can get intense. I've never really been the one-night-stand type. But you looked so…*juicy* at the grocery store, I couldn't help but wonder what you looked like without your clothes." He lifts an eyebrow but his eyelids lower. "I figured the worst you could do was reject me. You seemed nice based on the way you talked to the other customers. We both like the same snacks. I didn't see any harm in taking a chance. I really told myself that I didn't have to fall in love with everyone I had sex with. If you were interested, get in, get out, move on."

"And then we did what we did."

"Indeed," he replied. "And it was…" his eyes slide closed as he bites his bottom lip, shaking his head slowly. "Indescribably excellent. I've never…" he shakes his head faster and finally opens his eyes and looks at me. "The point is, I was already emotionally entangled from our meeting at IGA. Then I realized you put the last of the cheese in my bag and my heart practically exploded. But for ethical reasons, of course, I felt the need to go back and pay for what I'd taken. And I was driving past on my way back to my cabin when I saw you on the porch. That little kid inside me who loves fantasy and believes in fate couldn't ignore that. That was too much of a coincidence. So when I came over and you just flat-out asked me...what else could I have said? What else could I have done?" Comically, he gives an exaggerated lift of one shoulder and one palm, looking like a half of a shrugging emoji.

My face gets hot at the mention of my question, even as a laugh escapes me.

"Afterwards, I immediately went and called my therapist because it felt like you and me had gone through everything I experienced with Karen over the course of two years in the span of less than a day. The past week, I've been meeting with her every other day just to center myself and try to gain some perspective. Then when I got your message on the porch, the same old doubts sprouted up again."

I wince. I thought I was helping my

case and I just shot myself in the foot like a dumbass.

"It's okay. Just fear and baggage from a toxic situation in the past bubbling up. I know it sounds ridiculous, but I just saw that as another sign that we were meant to at least try together. Maybe it won't work out. Maybe we're too different or want opposite things or whatever. But I've been watching you build Reave Needers for years. I've admired what you've done for me, bringing me to the attention of a wider audience of readers and promoting my books by simply sharing how much you love them. My therapist and I have openly talked about how much I'd fallen for you over the years. I never knew your true identity, but I did message you pretty regularly. Unfortunately, I never get a response."

"When?"

He pulls his phone out of his back pocket, swipes on it a few times, and turns it to me. There, I see a message sent through the Reave Needers site. A message telling me what a great job I did with the AJC interview. Another about a funny blog post from last Friday.

I immediately bury my face into the

mattress, moaning in mortification while he laughs and gently rubs my back.

"I'm so sooooorrrrry!" I cry into the fabric that's so thick I'm almost suffocating in it. "I didn't know you were Scammereave!"

He chuckles again.

"Nice nickname. But I guess it makes sense now, why you never responded. Some rando claiming to be the exact person you built an entire fandom for starts messaging you directly out of nowhere. But why didn't you just block me?"

Finally, I roll over onto my back and he adjusts his soothing motion to my stomach.

"I...you were just so kind and encouraging. I guess it was nice to imagine that the real Reave could feel that way about me. It was a fantasy."

"Apparently not, though."

"True. Embarrassingly true."

"It's alright, Kasa," he says before kissing my forehead, making a relaxed warmth flow through me. "I can see how it must have looked to you. I just thought you were being your normally secretive self and didn't want to give up any hints to your identity by getting too chatty with me. But do you see what I mean now? I've been falling in love with you for the past four years, ever since I found out that Reave Needers existed. From the way you manage the site, to how you analyze my work so thoroughly, to the way you do your text interviews about me. It's like having a one-woman PR firm at my back. I've rarely been appreciated like that in my life. It was easy to fall for you even though I'd never seen your face, didn't even know your name."

Hearing him say he's been falling for me like I have for him makes my heart race. Though I was afraid it was irreparably shattered, I have my fantasy back. If he loves me and I love him, we can figure out all the rest later. I think. But I don't want to think. I don't want any more uncertainty or crossed wires. I want to *know*.

I hold his wrist, stopping his hand right on top of my belly button.

"One more thing," I say before sitting up. I scoot down to the edge of the bed and he follows suit, facing me with one foot on the ground and the other leg curled on the bed, knee pointing at my thigh. He looks a little worried.

I tell him everything. About Mom's cancer and my deferred departure, about asking for my job back at IGA after she got better, about Uncle Yuto's inheritance and Tory being in Atlanta waiting for me for the past three years. I don't gloss over Dillin and my recent conversations with Nurse Donova and Vanny about me being shy and passive. I want him to know all that, too. I finish with my determination to sleep on his porch until he had to talk to me tonight before he surprised me.

"I just...I want to be with you more than I want to breathe. But I'm scared that getting that wrapped up in you will... will..."

"Prevent you from becoming Kasa+?" he offers.

My shoulders drop as I give up the struggle to find the right words.

"Yes, exactly. I just want to be up front about the fact that, as much as I love you and as much as I want you, I can't give up on myself like that for you. I'd end up resenting you and not forgiving myself and I just..."—I choke on the thought— "I'd rather us part ways now as something like friends than fall into a trap like that."

That would be like once again getting everything I wanted out of life and having it ripped away. I'd rather not be teased like that. I'm hoping Reave won't put me in a position where I have to choose between him and my future. I get the guy, but lose myself? No. I deserve better.

Reave straightens his leg to slide his foot behind my back, then scoots closer to me, hugging my left shoulder against his hard chest.

"I can't promise I'll be the best partner, Kasa. I've got my shit to deal with, just like everybody else. The fuckery with Karen only went as far as it did because I didn't have the boundaries I needed to keep myself and our relationship healthy. Or end it before things got that bad. But one thing I'll never do is get in the way of you being happy. I'm all in with you, Kasa+."

Relief washes over me as I smile and he squeezes me close to kiss my cheek.

"So...I won't need to move to Louisville?"

"Not unless you want to. And I own two houses down in Atlanta. One of them is vacant now, so..." he shrugs. "I'll do what I can to be close to you while you figure things out. Like I said, I'm all in. Are you?"

I turn to face him, feeling tears of hope and gratitude burning behind my eyes, but trying to keep my composure. Now—with the air between us clear, everything out in the open, questions asked and fully responded to, our feelings for each other blatantly expressed—I'm more at peace than I've been since we met. Maybe more than ever in my life.

One hand pulling his face to mine and the other reaching to undo his belt buckle, I breathe my answer against his lips.

"Yes."

Acknowledgements

Thank you, reader, for buying / borrowing and reading *The Christmas Proof*. This is my first romantic novella without the elements of my writing that are normally present in my fiction work (maiming, psychological trauma, murder, etc.). If you came looking for something a little more calm and cute, I hope you found it within these pages and all my self-restraint was put to good use!

The Christmas Proof was an idea that popped into my head in October of 2023 while I was participating in NaNoWriMo. Since then, I've shared the concept, short samples, entire drafts, and art with people who are part of my writing community, which is made up mainly of the two critique groups that I attend and a smattering of supportive creatives on social media. While some provided piecemeal critique during writing group sessions, others (my alpha and beta readers) were brave enough to volunteer to read the entire manuscript to help me shape the book prior to publication.

I appreciate you all for your assistance and can't wait to work with you on the next project!

Atlanta Writes

Cara Davies

Eloise McCarthy

Khushi Saroha

Latrell R. Morris

Tawnya Weber

Terrica Taylor

Vicious Circle Writers Group

About The Author

Tenesha L. Curtis has been a lover of the dark, disturbing, and deviant since childhood. In her kindergarten and elementary school years, her favorite movies included classics like "Child's Play," "Problem Child," "Candyman," and "Adventures in Babysitting." As she learned to read, she finally broke away from Nancy Drew and Hardy Boys (at the behest of a middle school teacher) and delved into reading literature from artists like Toni Morrison, Edgar Allan Poe, Patricia Cornwell, Mildred D. Taylor, Alvin Schwartz, Ayn Rand, and Maya Angelou. Her fascination with the human psyche led her to earning a master's degree in addictions psychotherapy and working in the mental health world for over a decade. She uses this training and experience to influence straightforward books on writing made especially for newbie authors, and thrilling works of fiction in various genres. When she's not helping new writers develop their books for publication, she's teaching the next generation of scribes at events like the Atlanta Writers Club's Atlanta Self-Publishing Conference or the Editorial Freelancers Association's EFACON.

Keep up with her fiction, nonfiction, and other work in the publishing world by connecting with her online at ReadTenesha. com.